By Carrie Lara, PsyD

THE HEART OF MI FAMILIA

Illustrated by
Christine Battuz

Magination Press • Washington, DC
Amercian Psychological Association

To my husband, Roger, for your patience, love, friendship, and humor. You make me laugh, wipe away my tears, support my success and my failures, and keep me going when perhaps it looks just too hard. Te amo con todo mi corazon. To my children, Lilia and Leo, you are my continuing inspiration, hope, joy and the center of my world each and every day. To my mother for her constant strength, love and guidance, always being my teacher in life and more. I couldn't ask for a better Grandma for my little ones. And to my suegra, la Abuela to my children, who provides a perfect balance of warmth, cariñosa y amor, acceptance and silliness. - *CL*

À mon amie Caroline, de tout mon coeur xxx - *CB*

Books for Kids From the
American Psychological Association

Magination Press is a registered trademark of the American Psychological Association. Order books at maginationpress.org, or call 1-800-374-2721.

Book design by Rachel Ross
Printed by Sonic Media Solutions Inc., Medford, NY

Library of Congress Cataloging-in-Publication Data
Names: Lara, Carrie, author. | Battuz, Christine, illustrator.
Title: The heart of mi familia / by Carrie Lara ; illustrated by Christine Battuz.
Description: Washington, DC : Magination Press, [2020] | Summary: "A bicultural child describes her visits to her grandma's house and her abuela's house, and how both sides of the family come together to celebrate her younger brother's birthday"–Provided by publisher.
Identifiers: LCCN 2020000474 | ISBN 9781433832536 (hardcover)
Subjects: CYAC: Family life–Fiction. | Hispanic Americans–Fiction. | Racially mixed people–Fiction.
Classification: LCC PZ7.1.L3446 He 2020 | DDC [E]–dc23
LC record available at https://lccn.loc.gov/2020000474

Manufactured in the United States of America
10 9 8 7 6 5 4 3 2 1

In my home, two worlds become one.

My family is a mix of dos culturas, I am bicultural.

My mommy was born in the United States.

Her great **great** **great** **great**
grandparents traveled in boats from Europe to
North America a *really* long time ago!

My daddy was born in Central America. He came with his familia on a bus to Los Estados Unidos when he was a little boy, not so long ago. The bus ride took them two *whole* months!

There are lots of differences between my mommy's culture and my daddy's cultura, but lots of things are the same too.

My favorite time to visit mi abuela's house is in the summer. It's very sunny and warm, and we go for walks through the city to la playa to play in the sand.

Mi abuela has photos and artwork from her home country on the walls,

but she makes sure to have some space for my artwork too.

In la casa, everyone is talking
and laughing.
My brother and I run around
playing with our primos while
mis tios y tias are talking about
trabajos y politica.

The TV is always on, but no one is really watching, and mi abuela makes yummy bocadillos. I love the smell of tortillas cooking in the kitchen.

Abuela's house is

"el corazón de la familia."

The last time I visited we practiced singing feliz cumpleaños to mi hermanito for his birthday.

Shhh, don't tell him, it's a **surpresa**!

I love to visit my grandma's house in the fall
when all the leaves are changing colors.

Grandpa takes me and mi hermanito on tractor hay rides around the vineyard.

The house is filled with yummy smells of pumpkin, spiced apple cider, ham, and chocolate. Grandma and I love to work on art projects together, and sometimes I get to help in the garden.

When the family gathers at Grandma and Grandpa's, the house is full of noises. I can hear my aunts and uncles talking about work and politics.

My cousins and I run
around outside,
swinging on the rope swing
and riding bicycles.

Grandma's house is "**the heart of the family.**"

Last week, Grandma helped me make a special present for my little brother's birthday.

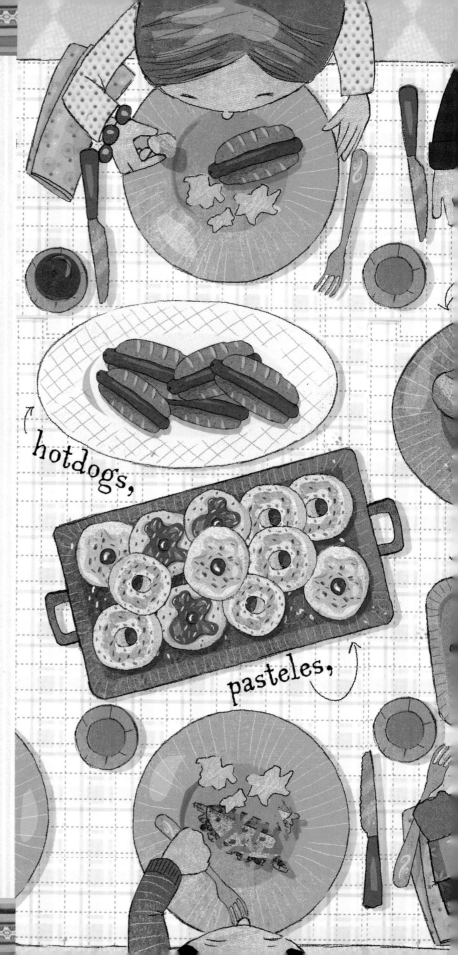

Sometimes we get to do things in one culture or the other, but every day I live in both.

Toda la familia and friends are coming over today for mi hermanito's fiesta! We have lots of food, all of our favorites...

hotdogs,

pasteles,

nacatameles,

liquados,

hamburgers,

tacos,

and ice cream!

We have a piñata filled with dulces, y juegos of bean bag toss and pin the tail on the donkey!

Grandma will bring a present for the little "handsome grandson" and Abuela will bring a regalo for the little "nieto guapo."

We will sing happy birthday in English and Spanish.

It is a very special celebration
for his cumpleaños!

En mi casa both of my cultures come together in a mixture that is

maravillosa!

The best times are when we are all together sharing in the joy
y amor that is our world, our blended cultura, our familia.

My world is lleno, full of experiences and richness.
I can't imagine my world in any other way, it is mine.

I am from dos culturas becoming one, I am bicultural.

Reader's Note

The Heart of Mi Familia follows a bicultural girl as she experiences the cultural differences between her grandma's home and her abuela's home. It highlights the wonder she has in her own bicultural life experiences and the joy and meaning that she finds in her daily interactions, activities, and routines. She describes her two "worlds" that come together beautifully and uniquely blending into one world within her home. Often people describe the experience of visiting other cultures or countries as visiting a different "world." It is the same world, only a different experience of life than that of their own. This feeling can be found as easily when visiting with friends or family of another culture, who may have different decorations, food, mannerisms, language, music, etc.

In both my professional career and personal family experience, children with two different cultural backgrounds can sometimes feel as if they live in "two different worlds." When they visit one side of the family they may feel like they do not quite fit in, and then have the same feeling when visiting the other side of the family. Sometimes people feel they have to reject one culture to belong to the other, which is then rejecting a part of themselves, suggesting something is wrong.

Research on cultural identity and immigrant populations has found that people can end up either in a state of acculturation, assimilation, or marginalization. In the attempts to join and find belonging, there can be a marginalization and rejection of the dominant culture, or assimilation which leads to a loss of the home culture. Acculturation is a balance of both, being able to adapt within the dominant culture for "survival," but also maintain a connection to the home culture. This is the healthy balance that we would want people to have.

However, children who have been able to develop this healthy balance can still have a feeling and experience of not quite belonging to one culture or the other fully. For example, when visiting family in Nicaragua, my husband's extended family will comment that his accent and language is that of a "Northerner." Although he was born in Nicaragua and Spanish is his first language, the influence of living in California has affected his language and mannerisms so that he sounds different. However, in California his English has an accent that notes him to not be a native-born Californian. Furthermore, his Spanish has an accent that is different than that of the majority Latino culture of the area in California.

There are ways as parents or caregivers that we can help our children appreciate and celebrate our own cultures, the cultures of others, and the beautiful diversity of our life experiences.

Acknowledging Differences

For children, as little social scientists, making observations of their surroundings and experiences every day is part of their learning and developmental process. When your child observes similarities or differences, acknowledge their observation and help them to learn and understand. Accept that there are differences, and not only note the differences exist, but discuss why. Is it because of religion? Is it because of regional food? This, in effect, discourages any developing thoughts or feelings that a difference in culture is wrong. It gives it meaning.

Supporting Your Child's Exploration

Children start to identify their own cultural/racial identity around the age of 3–4. This identification comes from the interactions they have with their family members, friends, teachers, and community. By age 7–9, children are more aware of the group dynamics around culture and race. This includes the histories of their own culture, and how their culture is similar, different, or a combination of other cultures.

This is even more important for children with multiple cultural histories. A child may at certain times in their life feel more identified with one or the other cultures in their background. This is part of their cultural experience and identity development. Be supportive and accepting of their exploration. By celebrating a child's unique individual culture and highlighting the beauty that both cultures can bring into their lives, you are celebrating the beauty of your child.

Talking About Cultural Identity

Have conversations about what culture is, and what cultural identity is. Cultural identity is made up of the multiple pieces that influence an individual's personal identity. These include the social construct of race, but also the person's language, food, music, family role, town, hobbies, profession, and so on. Relate that to yourself and to your child. A fun and easy way to help visually depict cultural identity is to create a list of what makes up your own cultural identity. For example, for myself: I am a mother, daughter, first born, older sister, wife, Euro-American descendent, English speaker, Northern Californian, children's book author, clinical psychologist, amateur singer, piano player, naturist, aspiring gardener, etc. Make a list for yourself and for your child, and note that throughout our lives this list may grow or shorten. Other proactive activities could be learning new recipes, language, or music and dance. There are lots of opportunities to highlight the beauty of culture all around us, from our own cultures to those of others.

Dealing With Discrimination

Unfortunately, our children will likely experience in one way or another conflict around racial tensions. Sometimes it can be overt, in the manner of comments, posted signs, or aggressive action. Or it can be covert, such as being excluded in a game on the playground, or dropped from a social group. Fostering positive conversations and development around cultural identity with your child builds a strong foundation of the cultural self and helps protect against these unfortunate experiences. When your child has a conflict, provide empathy and compassion, listen to and hold their emotions surrounding the situation. Let them express those emotions. Answer questions they may have with appropriate age level responses. Do what you can to protect them. This will differ by situation. It could be speaking with the school staff if something occurred at school, or with another parent if appropriate. Reassure your child it was not their fault, and they are not responsible for the actions of others. Remind them of their strength and beauty, and to celebrate who they are in and out.

As parents or caregivers, we are the best resource for helping our children respect and celebrate their own identities and those of others. We are our child's mirror and what we reflect back to them contributes a significant part to their perception of themselves, and their identities. We can help our children learn to value their own unique identities, and to find beauty and joy in the differences all around them.

Carrie Lara, PsyD, specializes in working with children and families on child and human development, including foster and adoptive youth, those with learning disabilities and special education, and children dealing with trauma, using attachment-based play therapy. Dr. Lara and her family share a love for culture and supporting her children in learning about their mixed cultural heritage. Through sharing in stories of her family, Dr. Lara hopes to support other families in having conversations about culture and diversity. She lives in Sonoma County, CA.

f @authorcarrielara

Christine Battuz has illustrated over sixty children books, including *Marvelous Maravilloso, My Sister Beth's Pink Birthday*, and *Shy Spaghetti and Excited Eggs*. Her work appears in educational books, magazines, toys, and toys packaging. She teaches art to adults and children of all ages. She lives in Bromont, Quebec.

Visit kuizin.com/illustration

Magination Press is the children's book imprint of the American Psychological Association. Through APA's publications, the association shares with the world mental health expertise and psychological knowledge. Magination Press books reach young readers and their parents and caregivers to make navigating life's challenges a little easier. It's the combined power of psychology and literature that makes a Magination Press book special.

Visit magaintionpress.org

f 𝕏 ⬤ 𝓅 @MaginationPress